Top
Cat

Top Cat

SCRITCH
SCRATCH

Lois Ehlert

Voyager Books
Harcourt, Inc.

Orlando Austin New York San Diego Toronto London

O-KA-LEE
O-KA-LEE

I'm top cat.
Pet me, I'll purr.

I guard this place
in my coat of fur.

PURR
URR
PURR
URR

Boring job! Never see a
Nothing much happens
in this dull house.

mouse.

CREEEK
SLAM

THUMP

SCRATCH
SCRATCH

Who let you in? One cat's enough.

ME-OW
SCRATCH
SCRATCH
SCRATCH
ME-OW

SNIFF
SNIFF

I don't want to
share my stuff.

SWISH
SWISH

SWISH
SWISH

Go away, cat!

GRRRR
HISS
HISS

You've
invaded
my space.

SWISH
SWISH

CHEEP
CHEEP
CHEEP

GRRRR
HISS
HISS

And I don't like your cute little face.

SWISH
SWISH

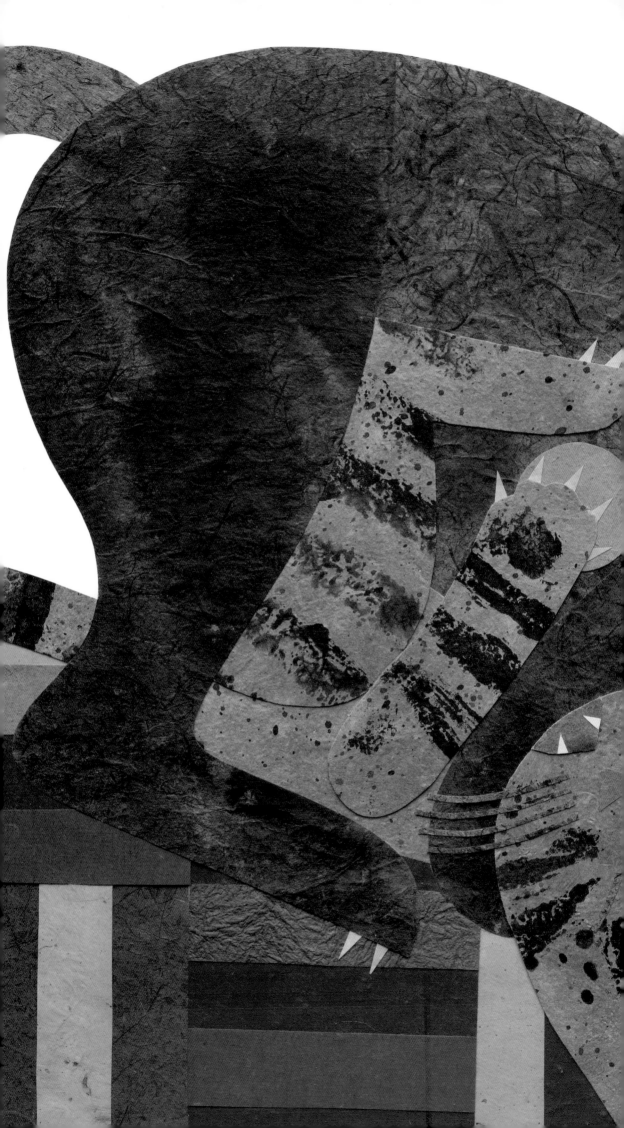

I'll fight you and bite
you behind the ear.
Get the message?
I'm boss
around here.

Well, you're here
to stay.
I can see that.

SCRATCH
SCRATCH

Guess I'm
stuck with you,
striped cat.

SWISH

JINGLE
JINGLE

THUNK

But
there's
more to do
than eat
and sleep.

JINGLE
JINGLE

WHIZ

Keep your
green eyes
open.
Watch me
leap!

Bounce on the couch. Leave lots of hair.

Eat leaves till
the plants are bare.

CHOMP

CHOMP

Drink from the sink wher

DRIP

company's there.

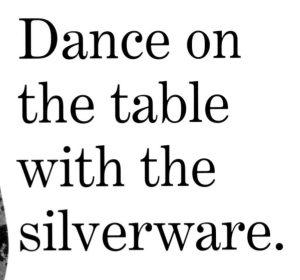

Dance on
the table
with the
silverware.

JINGLE
JINGLE

CLINK
CLANK

Door's
left open?
Go get
some
fresh air.

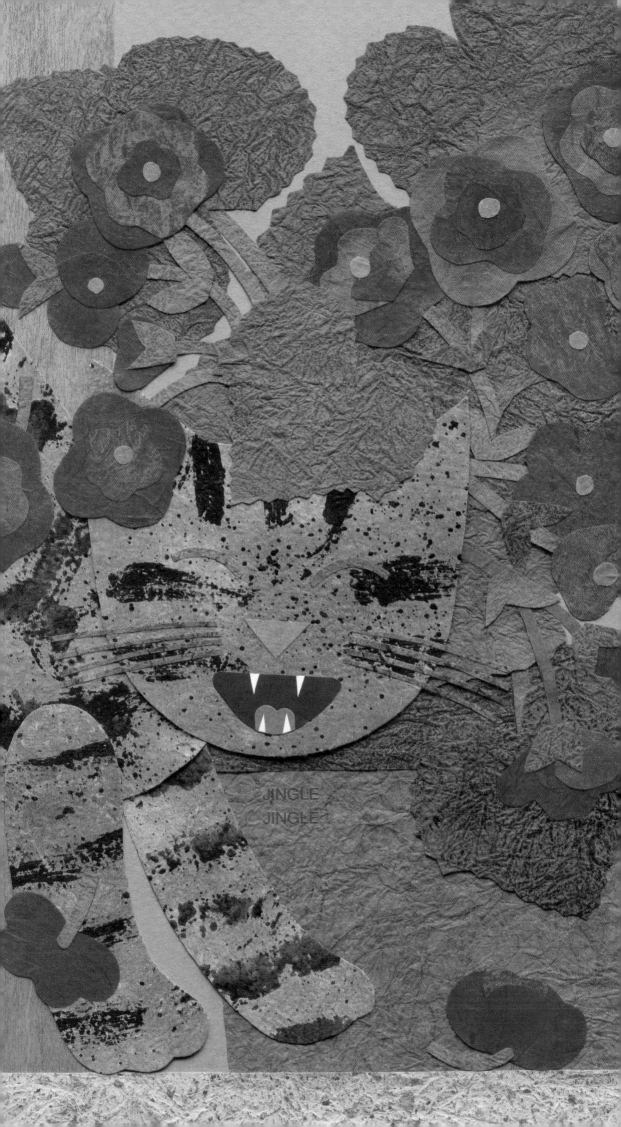

JINGLE
JINGLE

JINGLE
JINGLE

WHOOSH

Test your claws.
Give birds a good scare.

JINGLE
JINGLE

Time
to eat!
You'd
better
decide.

Will you come in
or stay outside?

WHAT
CHEER
WIT
WIT
WIT

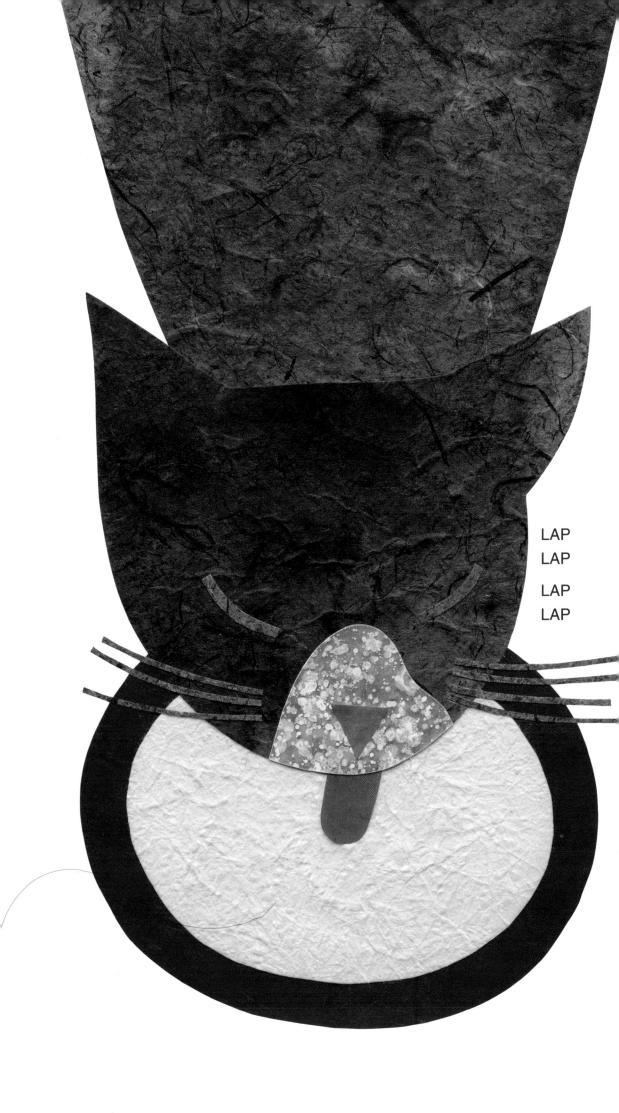

LAP
LAP
LAP
LAP

Welcome back!
Let's drink milk
in our furs.
No hisses,
no scratches,
no bites.

Just
purrs.

LIP
LIP
LIP
LIP

For Shirley and Don

www.hmhco.com

First Voyager Books edition 2001
Voyager Books is a trademark of Harcourt, Inc.,
registered in the United States of America and other
jurisdictions.

The Library of Congress has cataloged the hardcover
edition as follows:
Ehlert, Lois.
Top cat/Lois Ehlert [author and illustrator].
p.   cm.
Summary: The top cat in a household is reluctant to accept
the arrival of a new kitten but decides to share various
survival secrets with it.
1. Cats—Juvenile fiction. [1. Cats—Fiction. 2. Stories in
rhyme.] I. Title.
PZ8.3.E29To   1998
[E]—dc21 97-8818
ISBN 978-0-15-201739-2
ISBN 978-0-15-202425-3 pb

SCP 16 15 14
4500515541

Production supervision by Sandra Grebenar and Ginger Boyer
Printed in China by RR Donnelley, China

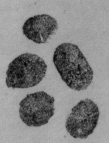